my cat
likes to hide
in
boxes

by Eve Sutton

Illustrated by Lynley Dodd

Parents' Magazine Press / New York

Copyright © 1973 by Eve Sutton and Lynley Dodd
First published in the United States of America
1974 by Parents' Magazine Press
First published in Great Britain 1973 by Hamish
Hamilton Children's Books Ltd.
All rights reserved. Printed in the United States of America

Library of Congress Cataloging in Publication Data
Sutton, Eve.
    My cat likes to hide in boxes.
    SUMMARY: Compares in cumulative verse the unusual
activities of cats from different countries.
    [1. Cats—Stories. 2. Stories in rhyme]
I. Dodd, Lynley, illus. II. Title.
PZ8.3.S989My3   [E]   73-12854
ISBN 0-8193-0752-1   ISBN 0-8193-0753-X (lib. bdg.)

MY CAT LIKES TO HIDE IN BOXES

The cat from France
Liked to sing and dance

But MY cat likes to hide in boxes.

The cat from Spain
Flew an aeroplane.
The cat from France
Liked to sing and dance.

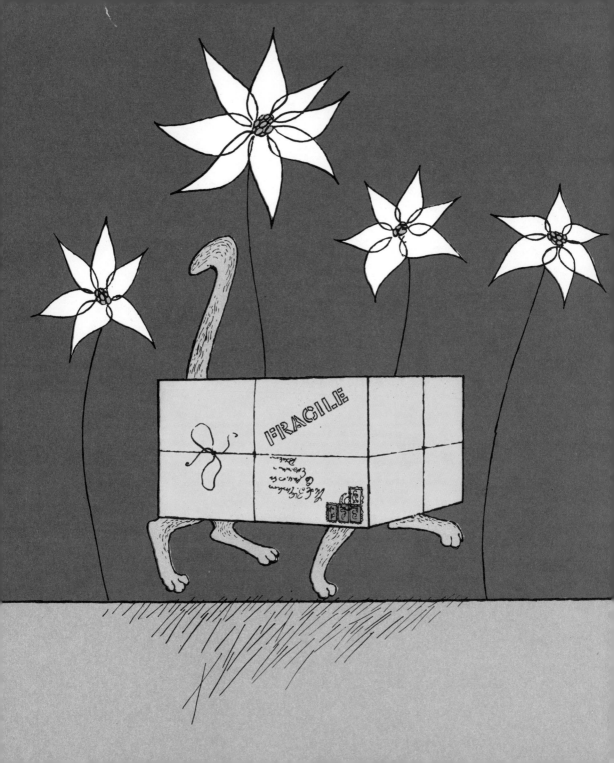

But MY cat likes to hide in boxes.

The cat from Norway
Got stuck in the doorway.
The cat from Spain
Flew an aeroplane.
The cat from France
Liked to sing and dance.

But MY cat likes to hide in boxes.

The cat from Greece
Joined the police.
The cat from Norway
Got stuck in the doorway.
The cat from Spain
Flew an aeroplane.
The cat from France
Liked to sing and dance.

But MY cat likes to hide in boxes.

The cat from Brazil
Caught a very bad chill.
The cat from Greece
Joined the police.
The cat from Norway
Got stuck in the doorway.
The cat from Spain
Flew an aeroplane.
The cat from France
Liked to sing and dance.

But MY cat likes to hide in boxes.

The cat from Berlin
Played the violin.
The cat from Brazil
Caught a very bad chill.
The cat from Greece
Joined the police.
The cat from Norway
Got stuck in the doorway.
The cat from Spain
Flew an aeroplane.
The cat from France
Liked to sing and dance.

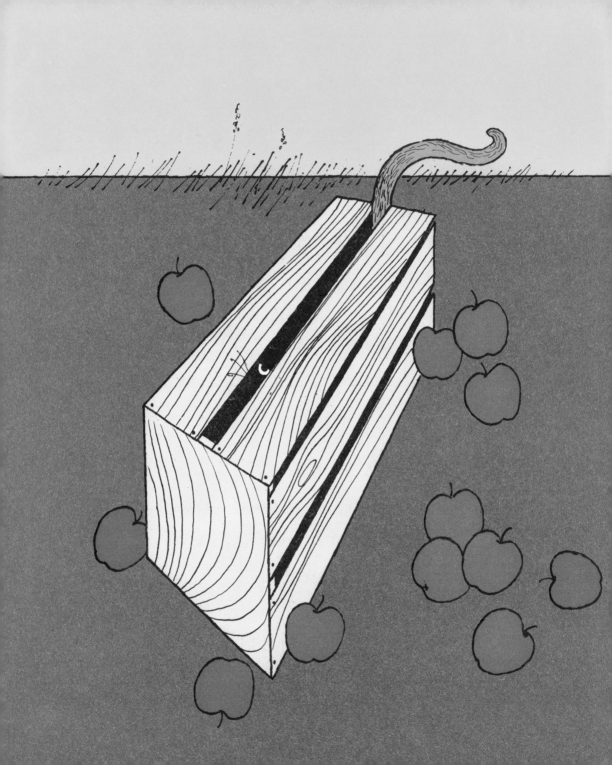

But MY cat likes to hide in boxes.

The cat from Japan
Waved a big blue fan.
The cat from Berlin
Played the violin.
The cat from Brazil
Caught a very bad chill.
The cat from Greece
Joined the police.
The cat from Norway
Got stuck in the doorway.
The cat from Spain
Flew an aeroplane.
The cat from France
Liked to sing and dance.

Look at all these clever cats,
Cats from Spain, Brazil and France,
Cats from Greece, Japan and Norway,
Cats who sing and fly and dance...

BUT MY CAT LIKES TO HIDE IN BOXES.